SAM'S
Wild West
SHOW

BY **NANCY ANTLE**
PICTURES BY **SIMMS TABACK**

DIAL BOOKS FOR YOUNG READERS
NEW YORK

Published by Dial Books for Young Readers
A Division of Penguin Books USA Inc.
375 Hudson Street / New York, New York 10014

First Edition
1 3 5 7 9 10 8 6 4 2

Library of Congress Cataloging in Publication Data
Antle, Nancy.
Sam's Wild West Show / by Nancy Antle
pictures by Simms Taback.
p. cm.
Summary: Sam and his Wild West Show entertain the townsfolk
and catch two bank robbers before moving on to the next town.
ISBN 0-8037-1532-3 (trade)—ISBN 0-8037-1533-1 (lib.)
[1. Cowboys—Fiction. 2. Cowgirls—Fiction.
3. Robbers and outlaws—Fiction. 4. West (U.S.)—Fiction.]
I. Taback, Simms, ill. II. Title.
PZ7.A6294Sam 1995 [E]—dc20 94-3358 CIP AC

The full-color artwork was prepared using pen and ink
and watercolor washes. It was then scanner-separated and
reproduced as red, blue, yellow, and black halftones.

Reading Level 2.1

*For two of my most favorite people in the whole world—
my daughter, Elizabeth, and my son, Ben*

N.A.

To Victoria

S.T.

Sam's Wild West Show

rode into town.

They came in buggies and wagons.

They came on horseback and on foot.

Everyone but Sam.

Sam flew into town in a hot-air balloon.

"This will be great!" the mayor said.

"Great," the banker agreed.

"I'll be sheep dipped,"

the marshal said.

Folks came from all over just to look.

Sam waved his hat at the crowd.
He landed his balloon and set up
his show in the middle of town.
Then Sam got on his horse and
cracked his whip. The show began!

CRACK!

A cowgirl rode standing up
on two horses.

A cowboy and cowgirl traded horses
while they were going very fast.

Sam rode with his head in the saddle and his feet in the air.

Everyone clapped.

"Great riding!" the mayor said.

"Great," the banker agreed.

"I declare!" the marshal said.

Next a cowgirl threw tin cans

in the air and shot them full of holes.

A cowboy shot wooden ducks

on a turning wheel.

Sam shot the tops off
twelve bottles of soda pop.
He did not break the bottles
or spill the soda.

Everyone clapped and cheered.

"Great shooting!" the mayor said.

"Great," the banker agreed.

"Forevermore!" the marshal said.

Finally a cowboy stood still.

He twirled a rope around himself.

A cowgirl twirled a rope while
she rode her horse around the ring.
Sam jumped rope
on top of a galloping horse.

Everyone clapped and cheered
and stomped their feet.

Sam bowed. Everyone loved Sam.

Sam cracked his whip again.

It was time for the GRAND FINALE!

The cowboys and cowgirls

got on their horses.

They all put flowers in their teeth.

"Stop the show!" a man shouted.

"I have a telegram for the whole town."

The man gave the telegram to the mayor.

The mayor read the telegram out loud:

"Outlaws headed your way STOP

Plan to rob your bank STOP

Warn marshal STOP

Good luck STOP"

The mayor's hand shook.

The banker turned green.

"We are in great trouble!"

the mayor said.

"Great," the banker said.

The marshal did not say anything.

"Where is the marshal?" the mayor asked.

"Gone," Sam said. "That way."

Sam pointed to a cloud of dust

that was headed out of town.

The mayor's teeth chattered.

The banker's knees knocked together.

"We need a new marshal," the mayor said.

The banker nodded.

"Sam!" the crowd shouted. Sam bowed.

The mayor pinned a badge on Sam.

"Hurray!" the crowd shouted.

The mayor and the banker ran to
the mayor's office and slammed the door.

Everyone else ran away too.

Doors slammed up and down the street.

Shades were pulled. Locks were locked.

The cowboys and cowgirls looked at Sam.

"Hide," Sam told them.

"I will call you when I need you."

Sam pulled up a chair
on the jailhouse porch.
He leaned back in his chair
with his whip in his lap.

He pulled his hat down over his eyes.

He looked like he was asleep.

"Oh, great!" the mayor cried.

"Great," the banker agreed.

Later two outlaws named Flo and Bo
rode into town.

They were ugly. They looked mean.

Even their horses looked ugly and mean.

Bo and Flo snickered
when they saw the empty streets.
They chuckled when they saw the bank.
They laughed out loud when they saw
the marshal asleep on the porch.

Flo and Bo broke down the bank door.

They stuffed two sacks with money.

Then they walked out the door.

They heard yelling.

Four people on two horses

were riding toward them.

Two men were sitting down.

Two women were standing behind them.

29

They rode back and forth.

The outlaws watched.

While they were watching,

two cowboys leaned over the bank roof

and roped the outlaws' guns.

Flo and Bo did not notice.

Suddenly the women jumped from their horses onto the outlaws' horses. They rode away fast.

"Hey!" said Bo.

"They are stealing our horses."

"Shoot them!" said Flo.

Their hands came up empty.

They each grabbed a bag of money
and ran down the street.
CRACK! It was Marshal Sam and his whip.
"Not so fast," he said.

Flo and Bo stopped in their tracks.

They put their hands in the air.

"Don't shoot," they cried.

Flo and Bo turned around.

"He's not holding a gun," Flo whispered.

"Run for it," Bo whispered back.

CRACK! CRACK!

The bags of money went sailing
back into the bank.

Bo and Flo looked at their empty hands.

While they were looking,

Marshal Sam roped them.

He tied them to the flagpole.

The mayor and the banker came out.

"You did a great job!" the mayor said.

"Great," the banker agreed.

Everyone else came out.

"Three cheers for Sam and

his Wild West Show!" someone shouted.

"HURRAY! HURRAY! HURRAY!"

Sam tipped his hat and bowed.

Then he handed his badge

back to the mayor.

The mayor did not know what to say.

Neither did the banker.

"We have a show to do

in the next town," Sam said.

Sam's Wild West Show left town.

They left in buggies and wagons.

They left on horseback and on foot.

And Sam flew off into the sunset
in his hot-air balloon.